THIS BOOK BELONGS TO:

_____

Isabella wakes up early to go to school. She is grateful that her eyes open up. Isabella sees the sun shining in her window. She takes a shower, brushes her teeth, and gets dressed.

Isabella hugs her teddy bear, grabs her special balloon, and goes to the kitchen to pick up the lunchbox her Mother left for her and puts it inside of her special balloon.

She kisses her Mother goodbye, opens the kitchen door, and walks outside to wait for the school bus. The bus arrives.

Isabella gets on the bus. She says good morning to the bus driver. She goes and sits next to KJ. KJ looks sad. Isabella said,

"I KNOW WHAT TO DO!"

Isabella asks KJ what was wrong? KJ said, "his Mom forgot to put his favorite race car in his blue backpack." Isabella reaches into her balloon, pulls out a race car and gives it to KJ. KJ is smiling. Isabella made KJ

HAPPY.

Now the bus arrived at school. Isabella gets off the bus with the other students. She walks down the hallway and sees Lisa on the floor, holding her knee crying. Isabella said,

"I KNOW WHAT TO DO!"

Isabella asks Lisa what's wrong? Lisa told Isabella she fell and hurt her knee. Isabella reaches into her balloon, pulls out a Band-aid and lollipop, puts the band-aid on Lisa's knee and hands Lisa a lollipop. Lisa is smiling Isabella made Lisa

HAPPY.

Isabella says goodbye to Lisa and walks to class. When she gets there, she says hello to the teacher and notices Sue on the floor with her favorite toys, looking sad. Isabella said,

"I KNOW WHAT TO DO!"

CLASSROOM 3

Isabella asks Sue what was wrong? Sue told Isabella that she broke her doll baby and could not put the doll's arm back together. Isabella reaches into her balloon and pulls out a new doll baby and gives it to Sue. Sue is smiling. Isabella made Sue

HAPPY.

It is now lunchtime, and the lunch bell rings. Isabella walks to the lunchroom and sees Mark. Mark is at the table crying. Isabella said,

"I KNOW WHAT TO DO!"

Isabella asks Mark what's wrong? Mark told Isabella that his Dad forgot to put his favorite sandwich in his lunchbox. Isabella reaches into her balloon and pulls out Mark's favorite sandwich and gives it to him. Mark is smiling. Isabella made Mark

HAPPY.

At lunch, Isabella had too much to drink and needs to use the bathroom. Isabella goes and uses the bathroom. While washing her hands, she hears Kelly crying. Isabella said,

"I KNOW WHAT TO DO!"

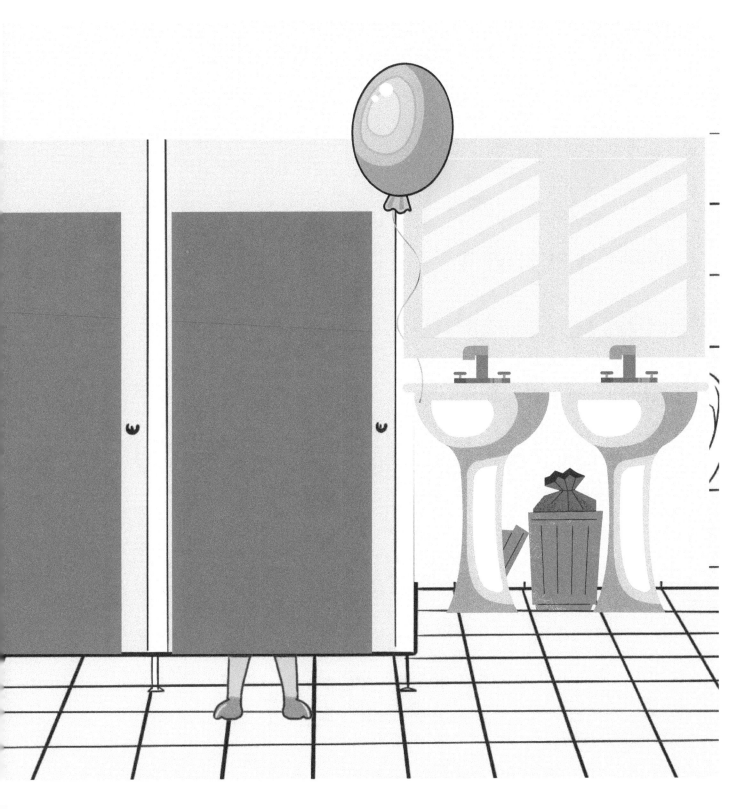

Isabella asks Kelly what's wrong? Kelly said, "she was using the bathroom and wet her pants." Isabella reaches into her balloon, pulls out a new pair of pants, and gives them to Kelly. Kelly now has on new pants. Kelly smiles and hugs Isabella. Isabella made Kelly

HAPPY.

While Isabella is in the bathroom, the bell rings. It is now 2:45 pm. It is time for Isabella to go home. Isabella walks outside to wait for her Mom to pick her up. When she sees Pam standing in front of the school, crying. Isabella said,

"I KNOW WHAT TO DO!"

Isabella asks Pam what's wrong? Pam told Isabella her teacher gave her an apple, and she dropped it on the ground. Isabella reaches into her balloon and pulls out a new apple and gives it to Pam Pam is smiling. Isabella made Pam

HAPPY.

Oh No! After helping Pam, Isabella looks up and sees snow falling. She knows that snow will pop her special balloon. Isabella said,

"I KNOW WHAT TO DO!"

Isabella reaches into her balloon, pulls out an umbrella and covers up her special balloon, as the snow begins to fall. Isabella is smiling. Isabella is

HAPPY.

Now Isabella is home safe, with her special balloon. She takes off her dirty clothes, takes a bath, brushes her teeth, and gets ready for bed. Her Mom comes into her room to tuck her in and kisses her

GOODNIGHT.

Isabella's Mom asked her what she did at school. Isabella told her Mom that she was a big helper and helped everyone in need, just like JESUS did. Isabella's Mom is smiling. Isabella made her Mom

HAPPY.

Isabella said her prayers and went to sleep.

THE END